The Taker Lady and The Giver Lady

Renee Eller

XULON PRESS

Xulon Press
2301 Lucien Way #415
Maitland, FL 32751
407.339.4217
www.xulonpress.com

Paperback ISBN-13: 978-1-6628-2352-7

Hardcover ISBN-13: 978-1-6628-2570-5

Ebook ISBN-13: 978-1-6628-2353-4

Dedication

This story was written for all my children and grandchildren.

I also want to give a very special thank-you to my husband, Dave, for his unwavering love and support, as I remember to always give God the glory.

Acknowledgments

Special thanks to a precious little girl named Willow and her parents for allowing me to borrow her beautiful name to tell my story.

Willow will forever hold a very special place in my heart.

The Taker Lady and The Giver Lady

Once there was a little girl named Willow, enjoying a lovely walk in the country when she came upon a fork in the road.

Willow looked up to see two ladies, dressed very similar in their outer appearances standing on each side of the forked road.

UNKIND UNKIND UNKIND
UNKIND UNKIND UNKIND
UNKIND UNKIND UNKIND

As Willow walked closer to the two ladies, she heard the lady on the left grumble.

Willow asked her what her name was, and the lady completely ignored her question. She started asking her OWN questions instead.

The lady replied, "You may not have passage on MY road until you give me something, little girl. Do you have an umbrella? I might get wet from a nasty rain. Hopefully you have a scarf because I hate getting cold during the night. Surely, you at least have some fruit, so I won't starve MYSELF down to MY bones out here guarding MY road!"

Little Willow just looked down at her tiny, empty hands in sadness.

Then, Willow looked up to the lady on the right and saw the lady smile at her.

She introduced herself as Miss Givens.

Miss Givens said, "Here, sweet child, please take this umbrella to keep you dry. For you never know when our God will open His beautiful sky with showers of blessings to help our gardens grow and our flowers bloom. Also, please take this lovely scarf, for I pray God will make the night cooler so His animals may rest more peacefully. Lastly, please take this delicious fruit so you will not be hungry on your lovely walk."

Willow knew only one name of the two ladies now, but not the other. So, she decided to call them "THE TAKER LADY" and "THE GIVER LADY," as she folded her tiny, little hands to pray.

Willow asked God to please help her with this fork in the road and give her guidance on what to do.

As Willow looked up, she couldn't help but notice that **"THE TAKER LADY"** did not smile and constantly grumbled. Willow could only understand the words, "Me, Myself and I" as the lady continued to complain.

But "THE GIVER LADY" had a most lovely and kind smile, as she continued to show her giving and thankful heart.

She told Willow, "We mustn't ever judge this grumbling lady, though she chooses her place in this life. I know that I never shall take it personally when she says I just act too kind. You see, my child, I know her problem isn't really with me but, sadly, her OWN reflection in HER mirror of life. So, we must always show her kindness and give her our love, as we continue to pray for her."

Then, Willow smiled as she accepted the lovely offerings from her new friend, "THE GIVER LADY," and turned to "THE TAKER LADY" with her tiny, little hands lifted high in the air towards this unkind soul.

She said, "Will you please take this new umbrella to keep you dry, as I have prayed for God to open His sky with showers of blessings to help our gardens grow and our flowers bloom? Also, I hope you will accept this pretty scarf to keep you warm, as I have prayed God will bring cooler temperatures so His animals may rest better tonight. Before I forget, please take this delicious fruit, as I have prayed God will use it to feed and nourish your soul."

Of course, "THE TAKER LADY" quickly grabbed HER new things and put them in the huge pile with the rest of HER other material things she had taken in life!

Then, Willow smiled and took the "RIGHT PATH"
to continue her life's journey.

THE END

May Compassion Write
Your Story
And Kindness Be
Your Signature.

A Note From The Author

After writing and publishing my first faith-based book, *The Reflection of Grace*, I decided to follow my dream of writing a children's book. I wanted my second publishing to also be a faith-based book and, after praying about this next adventure, I decided to listen to God and share my heart on paper once again. I am so thankful that with His guidance, I wrote this story for my family with a very prayerful heart. I also pray that it might open the hearts and minds of all children given the opportunity to read it.

As a Christian wife, mother, and grandmother, I deeply believe in kindness.

Because of this, I have always made it an important teaching in our home with our huge family of blessings.

This I know for sure: When we share our goodness with those around us, we can work together to change the world.

Always stay humble and kind.
Love and prayers,
Renee Eller

CPSIA information can be obtained
at www.ICGtesting.com
Printed in the USA
BVHW021336310821
615690BV00010B/830